Quotable Alice

From the works of Lewis Carroll

Compiled & Edited by

David W. Barber

The Quotable Press

Quotable Alice

From the works of Lewis Carroll

Compiled & Edited by
David W. Barber
Illustrations by
Sir John Tenniel

The Quotable Press

Introduction

The enchanting tale of Alice following a White Rabbit into Wonderland began as a story told aloud to amuse a real little girl, Alice Pleasance Liddell, and her two sisters during a boating picnic on the River Thames one summer afternoon in Oxford, England, in 1862.

Later, the Rev. Charles Lutwidge Dodgson – a shy, stammering mathematician and Oxford don – wrote down the story, calling it *Alice's Adventures Under Ground.* That simple, handmade original later came to be published, under the pen name Lewis Carroll, as *Alice's Adventures in Wonderland.* For the formal publication, by Macmillan in 1865, Dodgson's own rudimentary sketches were replaced by the now-familiar and much more detailed pen-and-ink drawings of Sir John Tenniel. (For a more detailed biography of Lewis Carroll, see page 107.)

Since that remarkable "golden afternoon," Carroll's two great Alice stories – *Alice in Wonderland* (as it's now more commonly known) and its 1871 sequel, *Through the Looking-Glass* – have entertained and amused both small children and grown adults alike for nearly a century and a half. (By happy coincidence, a different Alice had helped inspire *Looking-Glass*, eight-year-old Alice Raikes, whom he'd met in 1868 on a visit to his uncle Skeffington Lutwidge, in London.)

Though set in Victorian England, these wild, remarkable flights of fancy have a lasting appeal the world over and are, in many ways, surprisingly modern in their outlook. With Alice's adventures, which take her down a rabbit hole to Wonderland or through a mirror into a fantastical game of chess, Carroll tells stories that are absurdly amusing and witty, but also often surprisingly insightful and profound. (Even those who may not have experienced the Alice books as small children were often later to discover them during the usual adolescent period of existential angst. In that mindset, she fits right in.)

Many of Carroll's phrases and expressions – "Curiouser and curiouser," or "sometimes I've believed as many as six impossible things before breakfast" – have entered the language of everyday use (well, at least in some circles). With any luck, this little book may help that continue.

Alice herself has grown to become one of the most endearing, and enduring, characters in English literary fiction and dozens of other languages. This caused Carroll some chagrin, though it should not have been a surprise. Like other authors – Conan Doyle and his Sherlock Holmes being another notable example – Carroll turned out to be wrong about his own appeal. Like Doyle, he had hoped to be remembered for his more serious works – Doyle for his overblown historical novels, Carroll for his treatises on mathematics and logic. But posterity often has a way of making its own choices, on which authors are generally not consulted.

In compiling the most entertaining and memorable of these quotations, I've taken some liberties with their order, avoiding a strict chronology in favor of what I hope is a more interesting arrangement that groups similar quotes together to create a more appealing "flow" (though I've kept the two books separate to avoid unnecessary confusion). And if you need help finding a particular quote, there's an index at the back.

Readers may note how often Carroll returns to certain themes, such as learning, education and logic (he was, after all, a teacher) and of course their opposites (or is that corollaries?), namely absurdity and nonsense. There's much about word meanings and wordplay (witness Humpty Dumpty's imperious "When *I* use a word .."), manners ("Make a remark: it's ridiculous to leave all the conversation to the pudding!") and a surprising number about dismemberment and death. (When Alice tells Humpty Dumpty her age is seven and a half and "one can't help growing older," his reply is a little chilling, when you think about it: "*One* can't, perhaps," he says, "but *two* can. With proper assistance, you might have left off at seven.")

I've also taken the liberty, to a certain degree, of modernizing and simplifying some of Carroll's spelling and punctuation, generally just to make the excerpts easier to read. The most notable change comes in Carroll's eccentric rendition of *can't* and *won't* and similar words, which he spelled as *ca'n't* and *wo'n't*. (Technically, and logically, he's quite correct: the first apostrophe replaces the 'n' of can or the 'uld' of would, the second replaces the 'o' of 'not.' But however correct it might be, that spelling remains – somewhat like Carroll himself – overly fussy and pedantic. And besides, it never really caught on.) As Carroll might have said – it's too much like cant, and I won't have it.

My thanks go to Geoff Savage of Sound And Vision Publishing and *Quotable Books* for his faith in, and support of, this new Quotable series.

DWB
Toronto, July, 2001

All in a golden afternoon ...

All in a golden afternoon
Full leisurely we glide.

Wonderland,
Introduction

Alice was beginning to get very tired of sitting by her sister on the bank and of having nothing to do.

Wonderland,
Chap. 1, *Down the Rabbit-Hole*

So she was considering, in her own mind (as well as she could, for the hot day made her feel very sleepy and stupid), whether the pleasure of making a daisy-chain would be worth the trouble of getting up and picking the daisies.

Wonderland,
Chap. 1, *Down the Rabbit-Hole*

**She thought they were
nice grand words to say ...**

"Curiouser and curiouser!" cried Alice (she was so much surprised that for the moment she quite forgot how to speak good English).

Alice, *Wonderland*,
Chap. 2, *The Pool of Tears*

"*Un*important, of course I meant," the King hastily said, and went on to himself in an undertone, "important – unimportant – important – unimportant – " as if he were trying which word sounded best.

The King of Hearts, *Wonderland*,
Chap. 12, *Alice's Evidence*

She said this last word two or three times over to herself, being rather proud of it: for she thought, and rightly too, that very few little girls of her age knew the meaning of it at all.

Alice, *Wonderland*,
Chap. 11, *Who Stole the Tarts?*

"Speak English!" said the Eaglet. "I don't know the meaning of half those long words and, what's more, I don't believe you do either!"

The Eaglet, *Wonderland*,
Chap. 3, *A Caucus-Race and a Long Tale*

Alice had not the slightest idea what Latitude was, or Longitude either, but she thought they were nice grand words to say.

Wonderland,
Chap. 1, *Down the Rabbit-Hole*

"I'm sure those are not the right words," said poor Alice, and her eyes filled with tears again.

Alice, *Wonderland,*
Chap. 2, *The Pool of Tears*

"I think I should understand that better," Alice said very politely, "if I had it written down: but I can't quite follow it as you say it."

Alice to the Duchess, *Wonderland,*
Chap. 9, *The Mock Turtle's Story*

"And what is the use of a book," thought Alice, "without pictures or conversations?"

Alice, *Wonderland,*
Chap. 1, *Down the Rabbit-Hole*

"Oh dear, what nonsense I'm talking!"

"Well, *I* never heard it before," said the Mock Turtle, "but is sounds uncommon nonsense."

The Mock Turtle, *Wonderland,*
Chap. 10, *The Lobster-Quadrille*

"Oh dear, what nonsense I'm talking!"

Alice, *Wonderland,*
Chap. 2, *The Pool of Tears*

"If there's no meaning in it," said the King, "that saves a world of trouble, you know, as we needn't try to find any."

The King of Hearts, *Wonderland,*
Chap. 12, *Alice's Evidence*

"I shall do nothing of the sort," said the Mouse, getting up and walking away. "You insult me by talking such nonsense!"

The Mouse, *Wonderland,*
Chap. 3, *A Caucus-Race and a
Long Tale*

"Oh dear, how puzzling it all is!"

Alice, *Wonderland,*
Chap. 2, *The Pool of Tears*

"That *will* be a queer thing, to be sure! However, everything is queer today."

Alice, *Wonderland,*
Chap. 2, *The Pool of Tears*

"How queer it seems," Alice said to herself, "to be going messages for a rabbit!"

Alice, *Wonderland,*
Chap. 4, *The Rabbit Sends in a Little Bill*

"That's very curious!" she thought. "But everything's curious today."

Alice, Wonderland,
Chap. 7, *A Mad Tea-Party*

"It's rather curious, you know, this sort of life!"

Alice, *Wonderland,*
Chap. 4, *The Rabbit Sends in a Little Bill*

"Oh, how I wish I could shut up like a telescope! I think I could, if only I knew how to begin" For, you see, so many out-of-the-way things had happened lately, that Alice had begun to think that very few things indeed were really impossible.

Alice, *Wonderland,*
Chap. 1, *Down the Rabbit-Hole*

"What a curious feeling!" said Alice. "I must be shutting up like a telescope!"

> Alice, *Wonderland*,
> Chap. 1, *Down the*
> *Rabbit-Hole*

"For it might end,
you know, in my
going out
altogether,
like a candle."

"Well!" thought Alice to herself. "After such a fall as this, I shall think nothing of tumbling down stairs! How brave they'll all think me at home! Why, I wouldn't say anything about it, even if I fell off the top of the house! (Which was very likely true.)

> Alice, *Wonderland*,
> Chap. 1, *Down the*
> *Rabbit-Hole*

"For it might end, you know," said Alice to herself," in my going out altogether, like a candle. I wonder what I should be like then?" And she tried to fancy what the flame of a candle looks like after the candle is blown out, for she could not remember ever having seen such a thing.

Alice, *Wonderland*,
Chap. 1, *Down the Rabbit-Hole*

"Once upon a time there were three little sisters," the Dormouse began in a great hurry, "and their names were Elsie, Lacie, and Tillie, and they lived at the bottom of a well —"

"What did they live on?" said Alice, who always took a great interest in questions of eating and drinking.

"They lived on treacle," said the Dormouse, after thinking a minute or two.

7

"They couldn't have done that, you know," Alice gently remarked. "They'd have been ill."

"So they were," said the Dormouse. "*Very* ill."

The Dormouse and Alice, *Wonderland,*
Chap. 7, *A Mad Tea-Party*

It was all very well to say "Drink me," but the wise little Alice was not going to do *that* in a hurry. "No, I'll look first," she said, "and see whether it's marked *'poison'* or not."

Alice, *Wonderland,*
Chap. 1, *Down the Rabbit-Hole*

For she had read several nice little stories about children who had got burnt, and eaten up by wild beasts, and other unpleasant things, all because they *would* not remember the simple rules their friends had taught them: such as, that a red-hot poker will burn you if you hold it too long; and that, if you cut your finger *very* deeply with a knife, it usually bleeds.

Wonderland,
Chap. 1, *Down the Rabbit-Hole*

"That *was* a narrow escape!" said Alice, a good deal frightened at the sudden change, but very glad to find herself still in existence.

Alice, *Wonderland,*
Chap. 2, *The Pool of Tears*

She had never forgotten that, if you drink much from a bottle marked "poison," it is almost certain to disagree with you, sooner or later.

Wonderland,
Chap. 1, *Down the Rabbit-Hole*

"Maybe it's always pepper that makes people hot-tempered," she went on, very much pleased at having found out a new kind of rule, "and vinegar that makes them sour – and camomile that makes them bitter – and – and barley-sugar and such things that make children sweet-tempered."

The Duchess to Alice, *Wonderland,*
Chap. 9, *The Mock Turtle's Story*

"I suppose I ought to eat or drink something or other, but the great question is 'What?'"

Alice, *Wonderland,*
Chap. 4, *The Rabbit Sends in a Little Bill*

"Beautiful Soup, so rich and green,
Waiting in a hot tureen!
Who for such dainties would not stoop?
Soup of the evening, beautiful Soup!"
The Mock Turtle, *Wonderland,*
Chap. 10, *The Lobster-Quadrille*

"I do wish I hadn't drunk quite so much."
Alice, *Wonderland,*
Chap. 4, *The Rabbit Sends in a Little Bill*

"Oh my fur and whiskers!"

"Oh dear! Oh dear! I shall be too late!"
The White Rabbit, *Wonderland*,
Chap. 1, *Down the Rabbit-Hole*

It was the White Rabbit returning, splendidly dressed, with a pair of white kid gloves in one hand and a large fan in the other. He came trotting along in a great hurry, muttering to himself, as he came, "Oh! The Duchess, the Duchess! Oh! *Won't* she be savage if I've kept her waiting!"

Wonderland,
Chap. 2, *The Pool of Tears*

It flashed across her mind that she had never before seen a rabbit with wither a waistcoat pocket, or a watch to take out of it.

Wonderland,
Chap. 1, *Down the Rabbit-Hole*

"The Duchess! The Duchess! Oh my dear paws! Oh my fur and whiskers! She'll get me executed, as sure as ferrets are ferrets."

The White Rabbit, *Wonderland,*
Chap. 4, *The Rabbit Sends in a Little Bill*

"Oh my ears and whiskers, how late it's getting!"

The White Rabbit, *Wonderland,*
Chap. 1, *Down the Rabbit-Hole*

"I really must be getting home: the night air doesn't suit my throat.

The Magpie,
Wonderland, Chap. 3, *A Caucus-Race and a Long Tale*

**"So either way
I'll get into the garden ..."**

In another moment down went Alice after it, never once considering how in the world she was going to get out again.

Wonderland,
Chap. 1, *Down the Rabbit-Hole*

There were doors all round the hall, but they were all locked; and when Alice had been all the way down one side and up the other, trying every door, she walked sadly down the middle, wondering how she was ever to get out again.

Wonderland,
Chap. 1, *Down the Rabbit-Hole*

"How funny it'll seem to come out among the people that walk with their heads downwards! The antipathies, I think – "

Alice, *Wonderland,*
Chap. 1, *Down the Rabbit-Hole*

Alas! Either the locks were too large, or the key was too small, but at any rate it would not open any of them.

Wonderland,
Chap. 1, *Down the Rabbit-Hole*

She knelt down and looked along the passage into the loveliest garden you ever saw. How she longed to get out of that dark hall, and wander among those beds of bright flowers and those cool fountains.

Wonderland,
Chap. 1, *Down the Rabbit-Hole*

"So either way I'll get into the garden, and I don't care which happens!"

Alice, *Wonderland,*
Chap. 1, *Down the Rabbit-Hole*

But she could not even get her head through the doorway. "And even if my head *would* go through," thought Alice, "it would be of very little use without my shoulders."

Wonderland,
Chap. 1, *Down the Rabbit-Hole*

"What is his sorrow?"

"Come, there's no use in crying like that!" said Alice to herself rather sharply. "I advise you to leave off this minute!"

Alice, *Wonderland,*
Chap. 1, *Down the Rabbit-Hole*

"I wish I hadn't cried so much!" said Alice, as she swam about, trying to find her way out. "I shall be punished for it now, I suppose, by being drowned in my own tears!"

Alice, *Wonderland*,
Chap. 2, *The Pool of Tears*

"What is his sorrow?" she asked the Gryphon. And the Gryphon answered, very nearly in the same words as before, "It's all his fancy, that: He hasn't got no sorrow, you know."

Alice and the Gryphon, *Wonderland*,
Chap. 9, *The Mock Turtle's Story*

"You ought to be ashamed of yourself," said Alice, "a great girl like you," (she might well say this), "to go on crying in this way! Stop this moment, I tell you!"

Alice (to herself), *Wonderland*,
Chap. 2, *The Pool of Tears*

She generally gave herself very good advice (though she very seldom followed it) ...

She generally gave herself very good advice (though she very seldom followed it), and sometimes she scolded herself so severely as to bring tears into her eyes.

Wonderland,
Chap. 1, *Down the Rabbit-Hole*

"Begin at the beginning," the King said, very gravely, "and go on till you come to the end: then stop."

The King of Hearts to the White Rabbit, *Wonderland,*
Chap. 12, *Alice's Evidence*

"I don't see how he can *ever* finish, if he doesn't begin."

Alice, *Wonderland,*
Chap. 9, *The Mock Turtle's Story*

"Would you tell me, please, which way I ought to go from here?"

"That depends a good deal on where you want to get to," said the Cat.

"I don't much care where – " said Alice.

"Then it doesn't matter which way you go," said the Cat.

"– so long as I get *somewhere*," Alice added as an explanation.

"Oh, you're sure to do that," said the Cat, "if you only walk long enough."

Alice and the Cheshire Cat, *Wonderland,*
Chap. 6, *Pig and Pepper*

"Who are *you*?"

Once she remembered trying to box her own ears for having cheated herself in a game of croquet she was playing against herself, for this curious child was very fond of pretending to be two people.

Wonderland,
Chap. 1, *Down the Rabbit-Hole*

And so she went on, taking first one side and then the other, and making quite a conversation of it altogether.

Wonderland,
Chap. 4, *The Rabbit Sends in a Little Bill*

Yet what can on poor voice avail
Against three tongues together?
Wonderland, Introduction

"How puzzling all these changes are! I'm never sure what I'm going to be, from one minute to another!"

Alice, *Wonderland,*
Chap. 5, *Advice from a Caterpillar*

"But it's no use now," thought poor Alice, "to pretend to be two people! Why, there's hardly enough of me left to make *one* respectable person!"

Alice, *Wonderland,*
Chap. 1, *Down the Rabbit-Hole*

She stretched herself up on tiptoe and peeped over the edge of the mushroom, and her eyes immediately met those of a large blue caterpillar that was sitting on the top, with its arm folded, quietly smoking a long hookah and taking not the smallest notice of her or of anything else.

Wonderland,
Chap. 4, *The Rabbit Sends in a Little Bill*

"Who are *you?*" said the Caterpillar

This was not an encouraging opening for a conversation. Alice replied, rather shyly, "I – I hardly know, Sir, just at present – at least I know who I *was* when I got up this morning, but I think I must have been changed several times since then."

"What do you mean by that?" said the Caterpillar, sternly. "Explain yourself!"

"I can't explain *myself*, I'm afraid, Sir," said Alice, "because I'm not myself, you see."

Alice and the Caterpillar, *Wonderland*,
Chap. 5, *Advice from a Caterpillar*

"Dear, dear! How queer everything is today! And yesterday things went on just as usual. I wonder if I've changed in the night? Let me think: *was* I the same when I got up this morning?

But if I'm not the same, the next question is 'Who in the world am I?' Ah, *that's* the great puzzle!

Alice, *Wonderland*,
Chap. 2, *The Pool of Tears*

"You are old, Father William," the young man said
"And your hair has become very white;
And yet you incessantly stand on your head –
Do you think, at your age, it is right?"

"In my youth," Father William replied to his son,
"I feared it might injure the brain;
But, now that I'm perfectly sure I have none,
Why, I do it again and again."

"You are old," said the youth, "
one would hardly suppose
That your eye was as steady as ever;
Yet you balanced an eel on the end of your nose –
What made you so awfully clever?"

"I have answered three questions,
and that is enough," Said his father.
"Don't give yourself airs!
Do you think I can listen all day to such stuff?
Be off, or I'll kick you downstairs!"
Alice, *Wonderland*,
Chap. 5, *Advice from a Caterpillar*

"Who cares for *you*?" said Alice. "You're nothing but a pack of cards!"
Alice, *Wonderland*,
Chap. 12, *Alice's Evidence*

"Once," said the Mock Turtle at last, with a deep sigh, "I was a real Turtle."
The Mock Turtle, *Wonderland*,
Chap. 9, *The Mock Turtle's Story*

"You!" said the Caterpillar contemptuously. "Who are *you*?"
The Caterpillar to Alice, *Wonderland*,
Chap. 5, *Advice from a Caterpillar*

Alice had been to the seaside once in her life ...

Alice had been to the seaside once in her life, and had come to the general conclusion that wherever you go to on the English coast, you find a number of bathing machines in the sea, some children digging in the sand with wooden spades, then of row of lodging houses, and behind them a railway station.

Wonderland,
Chap. 2, *The Pool of Tears*

How doth the little crocodile
Improve his shining tail,
And pour the waters of the Nile
On every golden scale!

How cheerfully he seems to grin,
How neatly spreads his claws,
And welcomes little fishes in,
With gently smiling jaws!

Alice, *Wonderland,*
Chap. 2, *The Pool of Tears*

"How the creatures order one about ..."

They began running when they liked, and left

off when they liked, so that it was not easy to know when the race was over.

Wonderland, Chap. 3,
*A Caucus-Race and a
Long Tale*

"All I know is, something comes at me like a Jack-in-the-box, and up I goes like a skyrocket!"
Bill, the lizard,
Wonderland,
Chap. 4, *The Rabbit
Sends in a Little Bill*

"I never was so ordered about before, in all my life, never!"
Alice, *Wonderland*,
Chap. 9, *The Mock
Turtle's Story*

"It's really dreadful," she muttered to herself, "the way all the creatures argue. It's enough to drive one crazy."
Alice, *Wonderland*,
Chap. 6, *Pig and Pepper*

"It was much pleasanter at home," thought poor Alice, "when one wasn't always growing larger and smaller, and being ordered about by mice and rabbits."

Alice, *Wonderland*,
Chap. 4, *The Rabbit Sends in a Little Bill*

"How the creatures order one about, and make one repeat lessons!" thought Alice. "I might just as well be at school at once."

Alice, *Wonderland*,
Chap. 10, *The Lobster-Quadrille*

"We called him Tortoise because he taught us."

"When we were little," the Mock Turtle went on at last, more calmly, though still sobbing a little now and then, "we went to school in the sea. The master was an old Turtle – we used to call him Tortoise –"

"Why did you call him Tortoise, if he wasn't one?" asked Alice.

"We called him Tortoise because he taught us," said the Mock Turtle angrily. "Really you are very dull!"

The Mock Turtle and Alice, *Wonderland*,
Chap. 9, *The Mock Turtle's Story*

"Reeling and Writhing, of course, to begin with," the Mock Turtle replied, "and then the different branches of Arithmetic – Ambition, Distraction, Uglification, and Derision."

"What else had you to learn?"

"Well, there was Mystery." The Mock Turtle replied, counting off the subjects on his flappers – "Mystery, ancient and modern, with Seaography: then Drawling – the Drawling-master was an old conger-eel, that used to come once a week: *he* taught us Drawling, Stretching, and Fainting in Coils."

The Mock Turtle and Alice, *Wonderland,*
Chap. 9, *The Mock Turtle's Story*

"They were learning to draw," the Dormouse went on, yawning and rubbing its eyes, for it was getting very sleepy, Aand they drew all manner of things – everything that begins with an M –"

"Why with an M?" said Alice.

"Why not?" said the March Hare.

The Dormouse, Alice and the March Hare,
Wonderland, Chap. 7, *A Mad Tea-Party*

"I went to the Classical master, though. He was an old crab, *he* was."

"I never went to him," the Mock Turtle said with a sigh. "He taught us Laughing and Grief, they used to say."

The Gryphon and the Mock Turtle to Alice,
Wonderland, Chap. 9, *The Mock Turtle's Story*

"The best way to explain it is to do it."

The Dodo, *Wonderland*,
Chap. 3, *A Caucus-Race and a Long Tale*

"And how many hours a day did you do lessons?" said Alice, in a hurry to change the subject.

"Ten hours the first day," said the Mock Turtle: "nine the next, and so on."

"What a curious plan!" exclaimed Alice.

"That's the reason they're called lessons," the Gryphon remarked: "because they lessen from day to day."

Alice, the Mock Turtle and the Gryphon,
Wonderland, Chap. 9, *The Mock Turtle's Story*

**"You don't know much,
and that's a fact."**

"I'm older than you, and must know better."

The Lory, *Wonderland*,
Chap. 3, *A Caucus-Race and a Long Tale*

"You don't know much," said the Duchess, "and that's a fact."

The Duchess to Alice, *Wonderland*,
Chap. 6, *Pig and Pepper*

"When I used to read fairy tales, I fancied that kind of thing never happened, and now here I am in the middle of one!"

Alice, *Wonderland*,
Chap. 4, *The Rabbit Sends in a Little Bill*

"There ought to be a book written about me, that there ought!"

Alice, *Wonderland*,
Chap. 4, *The Rabbit Sends in a Little Bill*

It sounded an excellent plan, no doubt, and very neatly and simply arranged. The only difficulty was that she had not the smallest idea how to set about it.

Wonderland,
Chap. 4, *The Rabbit Sends in a Little Bill*

"If everybody minded their own business ..."

"There's no sort of use in knocking," said the Footman, "and that for two reasons. First, because I'm on the same side of the door as you are: secondly, because they're making such a noise inside, no one could possibly hear you."

> The Footman, *Wonderland*,
> Chap. 6, *Pig and Pepper*

"There might be some sense in your knocking," the Footman went on, without attending to her, "if we had the door between us. For instance, if you were *inside*, you might knock, and I could let you out, you know."

> The Footman, *Wonderland*,
> Chap. 6, *Pig and Pepper*

"How am I to get in?" asked Alice again, in a louder tone.

"*Are* you to get in at all?" said the Footman. "That's the first question, you know."

> Alice and the Footman, *Wonderland*,
> Chap. 6, *Pig and Pepper*

"I shall sit here," he said, "on and off, for days and days."

The Footman, *Wonderland*,
Chap. 6, *Pig and Pepper*

"Speak roughly to your little boy,
And beat him when he sneezes:
He only does it to annoy,
Because he knows it teases."

"I speak severely to my boy,
I beat him when he sneezes;
For he can thoroughly enjoy
The pepper when he pleases!"

The Duchess, *Wonderland*,
Chap. 6, *Pig and Pepper*

"You should learn not to make personal remarks," Alice said with some severity: "It's very rude."

Alice to the Mad Hatter, *Wonderland*,
Chap. 7, *A Mad Tea-Party*

"If everybody minded their own business," the Duchess said, in a hoarse growl, "the world would go round a deal faster than it does."

The Duchess, *Wonderland*,
Chap. 6, *Pig and Pepper*

"Really, now, you ask me," said Alice, very much confused, "I don't think –"

"Then you shouldn't talk," said the Hatter.

Alice and the Mad Hatter, *Wonderland*,
Chap. 7, *A Mad Tea-Party*

"Don't grunt," said Alice. "That's not at all a proper way of expressing yourself."

Alice to the Duchess's baby, *Wonderland*,
Chap. 6, *Pig and Pepper*

"If it had grown up," she said to herself, "it would have made a dreadfully ugly child: but it makes rather a handsome pig, I think." And she began thinking over other children she knew who might do very well as pigs, and was just saying to herself "if one only knew the right way to change them –"

Alice, *Wonderland*,
Chap. 6, *Pig and
Pepper*

It looked good-natured, she thought: still, it had *very* long claws and a great many teeth, so she felt that it ought to be treated with respect.

Alice on the Cheshire
Cat, *Wonderland*,
Chap. 6, *Pig and
Pepper*

"We beg your acceptance of this elegant thimble."

"I make you a present of everything I've said as yet."

"A cheap sort of present!" thought Alice. "I'm glad people don't give birthday presents like that!" But she did not venture to say it out loud.

"Thinking again?" the Duchess asked, with another dig of her sharp little chin.

"I've a right to think," said Alice sharply, for she was beginning to feel a little worried.

"Just about as much right," said the Duchess, "as pigs have to fly."

The Duchess and Alice, *Wonderland*, Chap. 9, *The Mock Turtle's Story*

Then they all crowded around her once more, while the Dodo solemnly presented the thimble, saying "We beg your acceptance of this elegant thimble'." And, when it had finished this short speech, they all cheered.

The Dodo, *Wonderland,*
Chap. 3, *A Caucus-Race and a Long Tale*

Alice thought the whole thing very absurd, but they all looked so grave that she did not dare to laugh. And, as she could not think of anything to say, she simply bowed and took the thimble, looking as solemn as she could.

Wonderland,
Chap. 3, *A Caucus-Race and a Long Tale*

Then they both bowed, and their curls got entangled together.

Wonderland,
Chap. 6, *Pig and Pepper*

She tried to curtsey as she spoke – fancy *curtseying* as you're falling through the air! Do you think you could manage it?

Wonderland,
Chap. 1, *Down the Rabbit-Hole*

"I didn't mean it!" pleaded poor Alice. "But you're so easily offended, you know!

Alice, *Wonderland,*
Chap. 3, *A Caucus-Race and a Long Tale*

31

"Why is a raven like a writing-desk?"

"In *that* direction," the Cat said, waving its right paw round, "lives a Hatter: and in *that* direction," waving the other paw, "lives a March Hare. Visit either you like: they're both mad."

"But I don't want to go among mad people," Alice remarked.

"Oh, you can't help that," said the Cat; "we're all mad here. I'm mad. You're mad."

"How do you know I'm mad?" said Alice.

"You must be," said the Cat, "or you wouldn't have come here."

The Cheshire Cat and Alice, *Wonderland*,
Chap. 6, *Pig and Pepper*

"You see, a dog growls when it's angry and wags its tail when it's pleased. Now, *I* growl when I'm pleased and wag my tail when I'm angry. Therefore I'm mad."

The Cheshire Cat to Alice, *Wonderland*,
Chap. 6, *Pig and Pepper*

"Why is a raven like a writing-desk?"
The Mad Hatter, *Wonderland*,
Chap. 7, *A Mad Tea-Party*

"Do cats eat bats, I wonder?" And here Alice began to get rather sleepy, and went on saying to herself, in a dreamy sort of way, "Do cats eat bats? Do cats eat bats?" and sometimes "Do bats eat cats?" for, you see, as she couldn't answer either question, it didn't much matter which way she put it.
Alice, *Wonderland*,
Chap. 1, *Down the Rabbit-Hole*

"Off with her head!"

Alice sighed wearily. "I think you might do something better with the time," she said, "than wasting it in asking riddles that have no answers."

"If you knew Time as well as I do," said the Hatter, "you wouldn't talk about wasting *it*. It's *him*."

"I don't know what you mean," said Alice.

"Of course you don't!" the Hatter said, tossing his head contemptuously. "I dare say you never even spoke to Time!"

"Perhaps not," Alice cautiously replied, "but I know I have to beat time when I learn music."

"Ah! That accounts for it," said the Hatter. "He won't stand beating. Now, if you only kept on good terms with him, he'd do almost anything you liked with the clock. For instance, suppose it were nine o'clock in the morning, just time to begin lessons:

you'd only have to whisper a hint to Time, and round goes the clock in the twinkling! Half-past one, time for dinner!"

Alice and the Mad Hatter, *Wonderland*,
Chap. 7, *A Mad Tea-Party*

"He's murdering the time! Off with his head!"

The Mad Hatter (quoting the Queen of Hearts),
Wonderland,
Chap. 7, *A Mad Tea-Party*

"Talking of axes," said the Duchess, "chop off her head!"

The Duchess, *Wonderland*,
Chap. 6, *Pig and Pepper*

"Off with her head!"
> The Queen of Hearts, *Wonderland*,
> Chap. 8, *The Queen's Croquet-Ground*

"Now, I give you fair warning," shouted the Queen, stamping on the ground as she spoke, "either you or your head must be off, and that in about half no time! Take your choice!"
> The Queen of Hearts to the Duchess, *Wonderland*,
> Chap. 9, *The Mock Turtle's Story*

The players all played at once, without waiting for turns, quarreling all the while, and fighting for the hedgehogs. And in a very short time the Queen was in a furious passion, and went stamping about and shouting "Off with his head!" or "Off with her head!" about once in a minute.
> *Wonderland*,
> Chap. 8, *The Queen's Croquet-Ground*

"It's all her fancy, that: they never execute nobody, you know."
> The Gryphon to Alice, *Wonderland*,
> Chap. 9, *The Mock Turtle's Story*

The executioner's argument was that you couldn't cut off a head unless there was a body to cut it off from, that he had never had to do such a thing before, and he wasn't about to begin at *his* time of life.

The King's argument was that anything that had a head could be beheaded, and that you weren't to talk nonsense.

The Queen's argument was that, if something wasn't done about it in less than no time, she'd have everybody executed, all round. (It was this last remark that had made the whole party look so grave and anxious.)

Wonderland,
Chap. 8, *The Queen's Croquet-Ground*

"They're dreadfully fond of beheading people here. The great wonder is that there's anyone left alive!"

Alice, *Wonderland,*
Chap. 8, *The Queen's Croquet-Ground*

**They were trying to put
the Dormouse into the teapot**

The table was a large one, but the three were all crowded together at one corner of it. "No room! No room!" they cried out when they saw Alice coming.

"There's *plenty* of room!" said Alice indignantly, and she sat down in a large armchair at one end of the table.

"Have some wine," the March Hare said in an encouraging tone.

Alice looked all round the table, but there was nothing on it but tea. "I don't see any wine," she remarked.

"There isn't any," said the March Hare.

"Then it wasn't very civil of you to offer it," said Alice angrily.

"It wasn't very civil of you to sit down without being invited," said the March Hare.

> Alice to the March Hare, *Wonderland,*
> Chap. 7, *A Mad Tea-Party*

Twinkle, twinkle, little bat!
How I wonder what you're at!
Up above the world you fly,
Like a tea-tray in the sky.

> The Mad Hatter, *Wonderland,*
> Chap. 7, *A Mad Tea-Party*

"Take some more tea," the March Hare said to Alice, very earnestly.

"I've had nothing yet," Alice replied in an offended tone, "so I can't take more."

"You mean you can't take *less*," said the Hatter. "It's very easy to take *more* than nothing."
The March Hare, Alice and the Mad Hatter,
Wonderland, Chap. 7, *A Mad Tea-Party*

"At any rate I'll never go *there* again!" said Alice, as she picked her way through the wood. "It's the stupidest tea-party I ever was at in all my life!"
Alice, *Wonderland*,
Chap. 7, *A Mad Tea-Party*

The last time she saw them, they were trying to put the Dormouse into the teapot.
Wonderland,
Chap. 7, *A Mad Tea-Party*

"I've often seen a cat without a grin."

Alice was rather doubtful whether she ought not to lie down on her face like the three gardeners, but she could not remember every having heard of such a rule at processions. "And besides, what would be the use of a procession," thought she, "if people had all to lie down on their faces, so that they couldn't see it?"

Alice, *Wonderland*,
Chap. 8, *The Queen's Croquet-Ground*

"I don't like the look of it at all," said the King. "However, it may kiss my hand if it likes."

The King of Hearts (about the Cheshire Cat),
Wonderland, Chap. 8, *The Queen's Croquet-Ground*

"I wish you wouldn't keep appearing and vanishing so suddenly: you make one quite giddy!"

"All right," said the Cat, and this time it vanished quite slowly, beginning with the end of the tail, and ending with the grin, which remained some time after the rest of it had gone.

Alice and the Cheshire Cat, *Wonderland*,
Chap. 6, *Pig and Pepper*

"Well! I've often seen a cat without a grin," thought Alice: "but a grin without a cat! It's the most curious thing I ever saw in all my life!"

> Alice, *Wonderland*,
> Chap. 6, *Pig and Pepper*

"A cat may look at a king," said Alice. "I've read that in some book, but I don't remember where."

> Alice, *Wonderland*,
> Chap. 8, *The Queen's Croquet-Ground*

"And the moral of that is ..."

"Tut, tut, child!" said the Duchess. "Everything's got a moral, if only you can find it."

> The Duchess to Alice, *Wonderland*,
> Chap. 9, *The Mock Turtle's Story*

"And the moral of that is – Oh, 'tis love, 'tis love, that makes the world go round!"

"Somebody said," Alice whispered, "that it's done by everybody minding their own business!"

"Ah well! It means much the same thing," said the Duchess, digging her sharp little chin into Alice's shoulder as she added, "and the moral of *that* is – 'Take care of the sense, and the sounds will take care of themselves.' "

"How fond she is of finding morals in things!" Alice thought to herself.

The Duchess and Alice, Wonderland,
Chap. 9, The Mock Turtle's Story

"Very true," said the Duchess: "flamingoes and mustard both bite. And the moral of that is – 'Birds of a feather flock together.' "

"Only mustard isn't a bird," Alice remarked.

"Right, as usual," said the Duchess: "what a clear way you have of putting things!"

The Duchess and Alice, Wonderland,
Chap. 9, The Mock Turtle's Story

"And the moral of that is – 'The more there is of mine, the less there is of yours.' "

The Duchess to Alice, Wonderland,
Chap. 9, The Mock Turtle's Story

"And the moral of that is – 'Be what you would seem to be" – or, if you'd like it put more simply –

"Never imagine yourself not to be otherwise than what it might appear to others that what you were or might have been was not otherwise than what you would have appeared to them to be otherwise.' "

The Duchess to Alice, Wonderland,
Chap. 9, The Mock Turtle's Story

**"We can do it without
lobsters, you know."**

"Change lobsters again!" yelled the Gryphon at the top of its voice.

The Gryphon, Wonderland,
Chap. 10, The Lobster-Quadrille

*" 'Tis the voice of the Lobster:
I heard him declare '
You have baked me too brown,
I must sugar my hair.' "*

Alice, Wonderland,
Chap. 10, The Lobster-Quadrille

"We can do it without lobsters, you know. Which shall we sing?"

"Oh, you sing," said the Gryphon. "I've forgotten the words."

The Mock Turtle and the Gryphon, Wonderland,
Chap. 10, The Lobster-Quadrille

*"Will you walk a little
faster," said the
whiting to a snail,
"There's a porpoise
close behind us,
and he's treading on
my tail."*
The Mock Turtle,
Wonderland, Chap. 10,
The Lobster-Quadrille

*"Will you, won't you,
will you, won't you,
will you join the
dance?
Will you, won't you,
will you, won't you,
won't you join the
dance?"*
The Mock Turtle, *Wonderland*,
Chap. 10, *The Lobster-Quadrille*

*"What matters it how far we go?"
his scaly friend replied.
The farther off from England,
the nearer is to France.
There is another shore, you know,
upon the other side.
Then turn not pale, beloved snail,
but come and join the dance."*
The Mock Turtle, *Wonderland*,
Chap. 10, *The Lobster-Quadrille*

"No wise fish would go anywhere without a porpoise."

"Wouldn't it, really?" said Alice, in a tone of great surprise.

"Of course not, said the Mock Turtle. "Why, if a fish came to *me*, and told me he was going on a journey, I should say, 'With what porpoise?' "

> The Mock Turtle and Alice, *Wonderland*,
> Chap. 10, *The Lobster-Quadrille*

"I could tell you my adventures – beginning from this morning."

"I could tell you my adventures – beginning from this morning," said Alice a little timidly. "But it's no use going back to yesterday, because I was a different person then."

> Alice to the Gryphon, *Wonderland*,
> Chap. 10, *The Lobster-Quadrille*

"No, no! The adventures first," said the Gryphon in an impatient tone. "Explanations take such a dreadful time."

> The Gryphon, *Wonderland*,
> Chap. 10, *The Lobster-Quadrille*

"Consider your verdict."

"Consider your verdict," the King said to the jury.

"Not yet, not yet!" the Rabbit hastily interrupted. "There's a great deal to come before that!"
The King of Hearts and the White Rabbit, *Wonderland*, Chap. 11, *Who Stole the Tarts?*

"No, no!" said the Queen. "Sentence first – verdict afterwards"
The Queen of Hearts, *Wonderland*, Chap. 12, *Alice's Evidence*

Fury said to a mouse,
That he met in the house,
"Let us both go to law:
I will prosecute you.
Come, I'll take no denial:
We must have the trial.
For really this morning
I've nothing to do.
The Mouse, *Wonderland,*
Chap. 3, *A Caucus-Race and a Long Tale*

Such a trial, dear sir,
With no jury or judge,
Would be wasting our breath
The Mouse, *Wonderland,*
Chap. 3, *A Caucus-Race and a Long Tale*

"I'll be judge, I'll be jury,"
said cunning old Fury.
"I'll try the whole cause,
and condemn you to death."
The Mouse, *Wonderland,*
Chap. 3, *A Caucus-Race and a Long Tale*

"I wish they'd get the trial done," she thought, "and hand round the refreshments!"
Alice, *Wonderland,*
Chap. 11, *Who Stole the Tarts?*

"The Queen of Hearts, she made some tarts,
All on a summer day:
The Knave of Hearts, he stole those tarts
And took them quite away!"
The White Rabbit, *Wonderland*,
Chap. 11, *Who Stole the Tarts?*

"If that's all you know about it, you may stand down," continued the King.

"I can't go no lower," said the Hatter: "I'm on the floor, as it is."

"Then you may *sit* down," the King replied.
The King of Hearts and the White Rabbit,
Wonderland, Chap. 11, *Who Stole the Tarts?*

At this moment the King, who had been for some time busily writing in his notebook, called out, "Silence!" and read out from his book, "Rule Forty-two. *All persons more than a mile high to leave the court.*"
The King of Hearts, *Wonderland*,
Chap. 12, *Alice's Evidence*

"It's the oldest rule in the book," said the King.
"Then it ought to be Number One," said Alice.
The King of Hearts and Alice, *Wonderland*,
Chap. 12, *Alice's Evidence*

"It seems to be a letter ..."

"I haven't opened it yet," said the White Rabbit, "but it seems to be a letter, written by the prisoner to – to somebody."

"It must have been that," said the King, "unless it was written to nobody, which isn't usual, you know."

The White Rabbit and the King of Hearts,
Wonderland, Chap. 12,
Alice's Evidence

"I shall be a great deal too far off to trouble myself about you: you must manage the best way you can."

Alice, *Wonderland*,
Chap. 2, *The Pool of Tears*

"How funny it'll seem, sending presents to one's own feet! And how odd the directions will look!
Alice's Right Foot, Esq.
Hearthrug,
near the Fender,
(with Alice's love).

Alice, *Wonderland*,
Chap. 2, *Pools of Tears*

"If you didn't sign it," said the King, "that only makes the matter worse. You *must* have meant some mischief, or else you'd have signed your name like an honest man."

The King of Hearts to the Knave of Hearts,
Wonderland, Chap. 12, *Alice's Evidence*

They told me you had been to her,
And mentioned me to him:
She gave me a good character,
But said I could not swim.

If I or she should chance to be
Involved in this affair,
He trusts to you to set them free,
Exactly as we were

My notion was that you had been
(Before she had this fit)
An obstacle that came between
Him, and ourselves, and it.

Don't let him know she liked them best,
For this must ever be
A secret, kept from all the rest,
Between yourself and me.

The White Rabbit, *Wonderland*,
Chap. 12, *Alice's Evidence*

"Oh, I've had such a curious dream!"

Alice had got so much into the way of expecting nothing but out-of-the-way things to happen, that it seemed quite dull and stupid for life to go on in the common way.

Wonderland, Chap. 1, *Down the Rabbit-Hole*

"Oh, I've had such a curious dream!"
Alice, *Wonderland*, Chap. 12, *Alice's Evidence*

So she sat on, with closed eyes, and half believed herself in Wonderland, though she know she had but to open them again, and all would change to dull reality.

Wonderland, Chap. 12, *Alice's Evidence*

Thus grew the tale of Wonderland:
Thus slowly, one by one,
Its quaint events were hammered out –
And now the tale is done.

Wonderland, Introduction

Through the Looking-Glass and What Alice Found There

Child of pure unclouded brow ...

Child of pure unclouded brow
And dreaming eyes of wonder!
Though time be fleet, and I and thou
Are half a life asunder,
Thy loving smile will surely hail
The love-gift of a fairy-tale
                                    Looking-Glass,
                                    Introduction

A tale begun in other days,
When summer suns were glowing –
A simple chime, that served to time
The rhythm of our rowing –

Whose echoes live in memory yet,
Through envious years would say "forget."

Looking-Glass,
Introduction

"It seems very pretty,
but it's *rather* hard to understand!"

"The horror of that moment," the King went on, "I shall never, *never* forget!"

"You will, though," the Queen said, "if you don't make a memorandum of it."

The White King and the White Queen, *Looking-Glass*, Chap. 1, *Looking-Glass House*

"My dear! I really *must* get a thinner pencil. I can't manage this one a bit: it writes all manner of things that I don't intend —"

The White King, *Looking-Glass*, Chap. 1, *Looking-Glass House*

'Twas brillig, and the slithy toves
Did gyre and gimble in the wabe:
All mimsy were the borogoves,

And the mome raths outgrabe.
"Beware the Jabberwock, my son!
The jaws that bite, the claws that catch!
Beware the Jubjub bird, and shun
The frumious Bandersnatch!"

He took his vorpal sword in hand:
Long time the manxome foe he sought –
So rested he by the Tumtum tree,
And stood awhile in thought.

And, as in uffish thought he stood,
The Jabberwock, with eyes of flame,
Came whiffling through the tulgey wood,
And burbled as it came!

One, two! One, two! And through and through
The vorpal blade went snicker-snack!
He left it dead, and with its head
He went galumphing back.

"And hast thou slain the Jabberwock?
Come to my arms, my beamish boy!
O frabjous day! Callooh! Callay!"
He chortled in his joy.

'Twas brillig, and the slithy toves
Did gyre and gimble in the wabe:
All mimsy were the borogoves,
And the mome raths outgrabe.
Alice, Looking-Glass,
Chap. 1, Looking-Glass House

"It seems very pretty," she said when she had finished it, "but it's *rather* hard to understand!" (You see, she didn't like to confess, even to herself, that she couldn't make it out at all.) "Somehow it seems to fill my head with ideas – only I don't exactly know what they are!"
Alice, Looking-Glass,
Chap. 1, Looking-Glass House

"We *can* talk, when there's anybody worth talking to."

"In most gardens," the Tiger-lily said, "they make the beds too soft – so the flowers are always asleep."
The Tiger-lily to Alice, Looking-Glass,
Chap. 2, The Garden of Live Flowers

"O Tiger-lily!" said Alice, addressing herself to one that was waving gracefully about in the wind, "I *wish* you could talk!"

"We *can* talk," said the Tiger-lily, "when there's anybody worth talking to."

Alice and the Tiger-lily, Looking-Glass,
Chap. 2, The Garden of Live Flowers

"And can all flowers talk?"

"As well as *you* can," said the Tiger-lily. "And a great deal louder."

Alice and the Tiger-lily, Looking-Glass,
Chap. 2, The Garden of Live Flowers

"Said I to myself, 'Her face has got *some* sense in it, though it's not a clever one!' Still, you're the right colour, and that goes a long way."

"I don't care about the colour," the Tiger-lily remarked. "If only her petals curled up a little more, she'd be all right."

> The Rose to the Tiger-lily, *Looking-Glass*,
> Chap. 2, *The Garden of Live Flowers*

"But that's not *your* fault," the Rose added kindly. "You're beginning to fade, you know – and then one can't help one's petals getting a little untidy."

> The Rose to Alice, *Looking-Glass*,
> Chap. 2, *The Garden of Live Flowers*

"Aren't you sometimes frightened at being planted out here, with nobody to take care of you?"

"There's the tree in the middle," said the Rose. "What else is it good for?"

"But what could it do, if any danger came?" Alice asked.

"It could bark," said the Rose.

"It says 'Boughwough!'" cried a Daisy. "That's why its branches are called boughs."

> Alice, the Rose and the Daisy, *Looking-Glass*,
> Chap. 2, *The Garden of Live Flowers*

"Never mind!" Alice said in a soothing tone, and, stooping down to the daisies, who were just beginning again, she whispered "If you don't hold your tongues, I'll pick you!"

There was silence in a moment, and several of the pink daisies turned white.

> Alice to the Daisies, *Looking-Glass*,
> Chap. 2, *The Garden of Live Flowers*

"Pudding – Alice: Alice – Pudding."

"Where do you come from?" said the Red Queen. "And where are you going? Look up, speak nicely, and don't twiddle your fingers all the time."

> The Red Queen to Alice, *Looking-Glass*,
> Chap. 2, *The Garden of Live Flowers*

"Make a remark," said the Red Queen: "it's ridiculous to leave all the conversation to the pudding!"

> The Red Queen to Alice, *Looking-Glass*,
> Chap. 9, *Queen Alice*

"Curtsey while you're thinking what to say. It saves time."

> The Red Queen to Alice, *Looking-Glass*,
> Chap. 2, *The Garden of Live Flowers*

"Open your mouth a *little* wider when you speak, and always say 'your Majesty.'"

> The Red Queen to Alice, *Looking-Glass*,
> Chap. 2, *The Garden of Live Flowers*

"Oh! Please don't make such faces, my dear! ... You make me laugh so that I can hardly hold you! And don't keep your mouth so wide open!"

Alice to the White King,
Looking-Glass,
Chap. 1, *Looking-Glass House*

"Pudding – Alice:
Alice – Pudding."

The Red Queen to Alice, *Looking-Glass*,
Chap. 9, *Queen Alice*

"It isn't etiquette to cut anyone you've been introduced to."

The Red Queen to Alice, *Looking-Glass*,
Chap. 9, *Queen Alice*

"Speak French when you can't think of the English for a thing – turn out your toes as you walk – and remember who you are!"

The Red Queen to Alice, *Looking-Glass*,
Chap. 2, *The Garden of Live Flowers*

"Don't keep him waiting, child! Why, his time is worth a thousand pounds a minute!"

The Insects to Alice, *Looking-Glass*,
Chap. 3, *Looking-Glass Insects*

"Better say nothing at all. Language is worth a thousand pounds a word!"

> The Insects to Alice, *Looking-Glass*,
> Chap. 3, *Looking-Glass Insects*

"Speak when you're spoken to!" the Queen sharply interrupted her.

"But if everybody obeyed that rule," said Alice, who was always ready for a little argument, "and if you only spoke when you were spoken to, and the other people always waited for *you* to begin, you see nobody would ever say anything ..."

> The Red Queen and Alice, *Looking-Glass*,
> Chap. 9, *Queen Alice*

"Always speak the truth – think before you speak – and write it down afterwards."

> The Red Queen to Alice, *Looking-Glass*,
> Chap. 9, *Queen Alice*

"If you think we're waxworks," he said, "you ought to pay, you know. Waxworks weren't made to be looked at for nothing. Nohow!"

"Contrariwise," added the one marked 'DEE,' "if you think we're alive, you ought to speak."

Tweedledum and Tweedledee to Alice, *Looking-Glass*,
Chap. 4, *Tweedledum and Tweedledee*

"You've begun wrong!" cried Tweedledum. "The first thing in a visit is to say 'How d'ye do?' and shake hands!"

Tweedledum to Alice, *Looking-Glass*,
Chap. 4, *Tweedledum and Tweedledee*

"I never saw such a house for getting in the way! Never!"

Alice, *Looking-Glass*,
Chap. 2, *The Garden of Live Flowers*

"It would never do to say 'How d'ye do?' *now*," she said to herself: "we seem to have got beyond that, somehow!"

Alice, *Looking-Glass*,
Chap. 4, *Tweedledum and Tweedledee*

"I beg your pardon?" said Alice.
"It isn't respectable to beg," said the King.

The White King to Alice, *Looking-Glass*,
Chap. 7, *The Lion and the Unicorn*

"If your Majesty will only tell me the right way to begin, I'll do it as well as I can."
Alice to the White Queen, *Looking-Glass*, Chap. 5, *Wool and Water*

"I'm glad they've come without waiting to be asked," she thought. "I should never have known who were the right people to invite!"
Alice, *Looking-Glass*, Chap. 9, *Queen Alice*

"Well, now that we *have* seen each other," said the Unicorn, "if you'll believe in me, I'll believe in you. Is that a bargain?"
The Unicorn to Alice, *Looking-Glass*, Chap. 7, *The Lion and the Unicorn*

"Is that all?" Alice timidly asked.
"That's all," said Humpty Dumpty. "Goodbye."

This was rather sudden, Alice thought: but, after such a *very* strong hint that she ought to be going, she felt that is would hardly be civil to stay.

> Alice and Humpty Dumpty, *Looking-Glass*,
> Chap. 6, *Humpty Dumpty*

"I shouldn't know you again if we *did* meet," Humpty Dumpty replied in a discontented tone, giving her one of his fingers to shake: "you're so exactly like other people."

"The face is what one goes by, generally," Alice remarked in a thoughtful tone.

"That's just what I complain of," said Humpty Dumpty. "Your face is the same as everybody has – the two eyes, so – " (marking their places in the air with his thumb) "nose in the middle, mouth under. It's always the same. Now, if you had the two eyes on the same side of the nose, for instance – or the mouth at the top – that would be *some* help."

> Humpty Dumpty and Alice, *Looking-Glass*,
> Chap. 6, *Humpty Dumpty*

"Of all the unsatisfactory people I *ever* met –"

> Alice on Humpty Dumpty, *Looking-Glass*,
> Chap. 6, *Humpty Dumpty*

**"You won't make yourself
a bit realler by crying."**

"Consider what a great girl you are. Consider

what a long way you've come today. Consider what o'clock it is. Consider anything, only don't cry!"

The White Queen to Alice, *Looking-Glass*, Chap. 5, *Wool and Water*

"You won't make yourself a bit realer by crying," Tweedledee remarked: "there's nothing to cry about."

Tweedledee to Alice, *Looking-Glass*, Chap. 4, *Tweedledum and Tweedledee*

"I know they're talking nonsense," Alice thought to herself, "and it's foolish to cry about it."

Alice, *Looking-Glass*, Chap. 4, *Tweedledum and Tweedledee*

"I liked it very much."

"I hope so," the Knight said doubtfully, "but you didn't cry so much as I thought you would."

Alice and the White Knight, *Looking-Glass*, Chap. 8, *"It's My Own Invention"*

"I could show you hills ..."

"*I've* seen gardens, compared with which this would be a wilderness."

The Red Queen to Alice, *Looking-Glass*,
Chap. 2, *The Garden of Live Flowers*

"*I* could show you hills, in comparison with which you'd call that a valley."

The Red Queen to Alice, *Looking-Glass*,
Chap. 2, *The Garden of Live Flowers*

"*I've* heard nonsense, compared with which
that would be as sensible as a dictionary!"
The Red Queen to Alice, *Looking-Glass,*
Chap. 2, *The Garden of Live Flowers*

"She runs so fearfully quick ..."

"Are we nearly there?" Alice managed to pant
out at last.
"Nearly there!" the Queen repeated. "Why, we
passed it ten minutes ago! Faster!"
Alice and the Red Queen, *Looking-Glass,*
Chap. 2, *The Garden of Live Flowers*

"Well, in *our* country," said Alice, still pant-
ing a little, "you'd generally get to somewhere else
– if you ran very fast for a long time as we've been
doing."

"A slow sort of country!" said the Queen. "Now, *here*, you see, it takes all the running *you* can do to keep in the same place. If you want to get somewhere else, you must run at least twice as fast as that!"

Alice and the Red Queen, Looking-Glass,
Chap. 2, The Garden of Live Flowers

"Would you – be good enough – " Alice panted out, after running a little further, "to stop a minute – just to get – one's breath again?"

"I'm *good* enough," the King said, "only I'm not *strong* enough. You see, a minute goes by so fearfully quick. You might as well try to stop a Bandersnatch!"

Alice and the White King, Looking-Glass,
Chap. 7, The Lion and the Unicorn

"No use, no use!" said the King. "She runs so fearfully quick. You might as well try to catch a Bandersnatch!"

The White King to Alice, Looking-Glass,
Chap. 7, The Lion and the Unicorn

"You might make a joke on that ..."

An extremely small voice, close to her ear, said "You might make a joke on that – something about 'horse' and 'hoarse,' you know."

The Gnat to Alice, *Looking-Glass*,
Chap. 3, *Looking-Glass Insects*

"If you're so anxious to have a joke made, why don't you make one yourself?"

Alice to the Gnat, *Looking-Glass*,
Chap. 3, *Looking-Glass Insects*

"You shouldn't make jokes," Alice said, "if it makes you so unhappy."

Alice to the Gnat, *Looking-Glass*,
Chap. 3, *Looking-Glass Insects*

"The time has come," the Walrus said ...

The sun was shining on the sea,
Shining with all his might:
He did his very best to make
The billows smooth and bright –
And this was odd, because it was
The middle of the night.

Tweedledee to Alice, *Looking-Glass*,
Chap. 4, *Tweedledum and Tweedledee*

'If seven maids with seven mops
Swept it for half a year,
Do you suppose,' the Walrus said,

'That they could get it clear?'
'I doubt it,' said the Carpenter,
And shed a bitter tear.
Tweedledee to Alice, *Looking-Glass*,
Chap. 4, *Tweedledum and Tweedledee*

'The time has come,' the Walrus said,
'To talk of many things:
Of shoes – and ships – and sealing wax –
Of cabbages – and kings –
And why the sea is boiling hot –
And whether pigs have wings.'
Tweedledee to Alice, *Looking-Glass*,
Chap. 4, *Tweedledum and Tweedledee*

'I weep for you,' the Walrus said:
"I deeply sympathize.'
With sobs and tears he sorted out

Those of the largest size,
Holding his pocket-handkerchief
Before his streaming eyes.

'O Oysters,' said the Carpenter,
'You've had a pleasant run!
Shall we be trotting home again?'
But answer came there none –
And this was scarcely odd, because
They'd eaten every one.
Tweedledee to Alice, *Looking-Glass,*
Chap. 4, *Tweedledum and Tweedledee*

"I'm very brave, generally ..."

Tweedledum and Tweedledee
Agreed to have a battle;
For Tweedledum said Tweedledee
Had spoiled his nice new rattle.

Just then flew down a monstrous crow,
As black as a tar-barrel;
Which frightened both the heroes so,
They quite forgot their quarrel.
Alice, *Looking-Glass,*
Chap. 4, *Tweedledum and Tweedledee*

"Of course you agree to have a battle?"
Tweedledum said in a calmer tone.

> Tweedledum to Tweedledee, *Looking-Glass*,
> Chap. 4, *Tweedledum and Tweedledee*

"I'm very brave, generally," he went on in a
low voice, "only today I happen to have a head-
ache."

> Tweedledum to Alice, *Looking-Glass*,
> Chap. 4, *Tweedledum and Tweedledee*

"We *must* have a bit of a fight, but I don't
care about going on long," said Tweedledum.
"What's the time now?"

Tweedledee looked at his watch, and said
"Half-past four."

"Let's fight till six, and then have dinner," said Tweedledum.

> Tweedledum and Tweedledee, *Looking-Glass*,
> Chap. 4, *Tweedledum and Tweedledee*

"Suppose they saved up all *my* punishments? ... What *would* they do at the end of a year? I should be sent to prison, I suppose, when the day came. Or – let me see – suppose each punishment was to be going without dinner: then, when the miserable day came, I should have to go without fifty dinners at once! Well, I shouldn't mind *that* much! I'd rather go without them than eat them!"

> Alice, *Looking-Glass*,
> Chap. 1, *Looking-Glass House*

"Perhaps Looking-glass milk isn't good to drink."

> Alice, *Looking-Glass*,
> Chap. 1, *Looking-Glass House*

"I hope no bones are broken?"

"None to speak of," the Knight said, as if he didn't mind breaking two or three of them.

> Alice and the White Knight, *Looking-Glass*,
> Chap. 8, *"It's My Own Invention"*

Alice thought to herself "I never should *try* to remember my name in the middle of an accident. Where would be the use of it?"

Alice, *Looking-Glass*,
Chap. 9, *Queen Alice*

"What a noise they make when they tumble! Just like a whole set of fire-irons falling into the fender!"

Alice, *Looking-Glass*,
Chap. 8, *"It's My Own Invention"*

"You know," he added very gravely, "it's one of the most serious things that can possibly happen to one in a battle – to get one's head cut off."

Tweedledee to Alice, Looking-Glass,
Chap. 4, Tweedledum and Tweedledee

"Crawling at your feet," said the Gnat (Alice drew her feet back in some alarm), "you may observe a Bread-and-butter-fly. Its wings are thin slices of bread-and-butter, its body is a crust, and its head is a lump of sugar."

"And what does *it* live on?"

"Weak tea with cream in it."

A new difficulty came into Alice's head. "Supposing it couldn't find any?" she suggested.

"Then it would die, of course."

"But that must happen very often," Alice remarked thoughtfully.

"It always happens," said the Gnat.

The Gnat to Alice, Looking-Glass,
Chap. 3, Looking-Glass Insects

"Seven years and six months!" Humpty Dumpty repeated thoughtfully. "An uncomfortable sort of age. Now, if you'd asked *my* advice, I'd have said 'Leave off at seven' – but it's too late now."

"I never ask advice about growing," Alice said indignantly.

"Too proud?" the other enquired.

Alice felt even more indignant at this suggestion. "I mean," she said, "that one can't help growing older."

"*One* can't, perhaps," said Humpty Dumpty, "but *two* can. With proper assistance, you might have left off at seven."

Humpty Dumpty and Alice, Looking-Glass,
Chap. 6, Humpty Dumpty

"Only we must begin quick. It's getting as dark as it can."

"And darker," said Tweedledee.

Tweedledum and Tweedledee, Looking-Glass,
Chap. 4, Tweedledum and Tweedledee

**"Jam tomorrow and jam yesterday
– but never jam *today*."**

"I'm sure I'll take *you* with pleasure!" the Queen said. "Two pence a week, and jam every other day."

Alice couldn't help laughing, as she said "I don't want you to hire *me* – and I don't care for jam."

"It's very good jam," said the Queen.

"Well, I don't want any *today*, at any rate."

"You couldn't have it if you *did* want it," the Queen said. "The rule is, jam tomorrow and jam yesterday – but never jam *today*."

"It must come sometimes to 'jam today'," Alice objected.

"No, it can't," said the Queen. "It's jam every *other* day; today isn't any other day, you know."

The White Queen and Alice, *Looking-Glass*,
Chap. 5, *Wool and Water*

"I know what you're thinking about," said Tweedledum, "but it isn't so, nohow."

"Contrariwise," continued Tweedledee, "if it was so, it might be; and if it were so, it would be; but as it isn't, it ain't. That's logic."

Tweedledum and Tweedledee to Alice,
Looking-Glass,
Chap. 4, *Tweedledum and Tweedledee*

"I don't understand you," said Alice. "It's dreadfully confusing!"

"That's the effect of living backwards," the Queen said kindly: "it always makes one a little giddy at first –"

Alice and the White Queen, *Looking-Glass*,
Chap. 5, *Wool and Water*

"It's a poor sort of memory that only works backwards," the Queen remarked.

The White Queen to Alice, *Looking-Glass*,
Chap. 5, *Wool and Water*

"Why, I've done all the screaming already," said the Queen. "What would be the good of having it all over again?"

The White Queen to Alice, *Looking-Glass*,
Chap. 5, *Wool and Water*

"There's no use trying," she said: "one *can't* believe impossible things."

"I daresay you haven't had much practice," said the Queen. "When I was your age, I always did it for half-an-hour a day. Why, sometimes I've believed as many as six impossible things before breakfast."

Alice and the White Queen, *Looking-Glass*,
Chap. 5, *Wool and Water*

"You couldn't deny that, even if you tried with both hands."

"I don't deny things with my *hands*," Alice objected.

"Nobody said you did," said the Red Queen. "I said you couldn't if you tried."

> The Red Queen and Alice, *Looking-Glass*,
> Chap. 9, *Queen Alice*

"There's nothing like eating hay when you're faint." ...

"I should think throwing cold water over you would be better," Alice suggested. ...

"I didn't say there was nothing *better*," the King replied. I said there was nothing *like* it."

> The White King to Alice, *Looking-Glass*,
> Chap. 7, *The Lion and the Unicorn*

"It's long," said the Knight, "but it's very, *very* beautiful. Everybody that hears me sing it – either it brings tears into their eyes, or else – "

"Or else what?" said Alice, for the Knight had made a sudden pause.

"Or else it doesn't, you know."

> The White Knight to Alice, *Looking-Glass*,
> Chap. 8, *"It's My Own Invention"*

"She's in a state of mind," said the White Queen, "that she wants to deny something – only she doesn't know what to deny!"

The White Queen to Alice (about the Red Queen),
Looking-Glass,
Chap. 9, *Queen Alice*

"With a name like yours ..."

"It can't be anybody else!" she said to herself. "I'm as certain of it as if his name were written all over his face!"

Alice on Humpty Dumpty, *Looking-Glass*,
Chap. 6, *Humpty Dumpty*

"With a name like yours, you might be any shape, almost."

Humpty Dumpty to Alice, *Looking-Glass*,
Chap. 6, *Humpty Dumpty*

"What's the use of their having names," the Gnat said, "if they won't answer to them?"

"No use to *them*," said Alice, "but it's useful to the people that name them, I suppose. If not, why do things have names at all?"

The Gnat and Alice, *Looking-Glass*,
Chap. 3, *Looking-Glass Insects*

"Some people," said Humpty Dumpty, looking away from her as usual, "have no more sense than a baby!"

> Humpty Dumpty to Alice,
> *Looking-Glass*, Chap. 6, *Humpty Dumpty*

"It is a – *most* – *provoking* – thing," he said at last, "when a person doesn't know a cravat from a belt!"

> Humpty Dumpty to Alice, *Looking-Glass*,
> Chap. 6, *Humpty Dumpty*

"It's a cravat, child, and a beautiful one, as you say. It's a present from the White King and Queen. ...They gave it me," Humpty Dumpty continued thoughtfully as he crossed one knee over the other and clasped his hands round it, "they gave it me – for an un-birthday present." ...

"What *is* an un-birthday present?"

"A present given when it isn't your birthday, of course." ...

"There are three hundred and sixty-four days when you might get un-birthday presents ... and only *one* for birthday presents, you know. There's glory for you!"

> Humpty Dumpty and Alice, *Looking-Glass*,
> Chap. 6, *Humpty Dumpty*

"When *I* use a word ..."

"Now I declare that's too bad!" Humpty Dumpty cried, breaking into a sudden passion. "You've been listening at doors – and behind trees – and down chimneys – or you couldn't have known it!"
"I haven't indeed!" Alice said very gently. "It's in a book."

"Ah, well! They may write such things in a *book*," Humpty Dumpty said in a calmer tone.
Humpty Dumpty and Alice,
Looking-Glass,
Chap. 6, *Humpty Dumpty*

"When *I* use a word," Humpty Dumpty said, in rather a scornful tone, "it means just what I choose it to mean – neither more nor less."

"The question is," said Alice, "whether you *can* make words mean so many different things."

"The question is," said Humpty Dumpty, "which is to be master – that's all."

Humpty Dumpty and Alice, *Looking-Glass*, Chap. 6, *Humpty Dumpty*

"They've a temper, some of them – particularly verbs: they're the proudest – adjectives you can do anything with, but not verbs – however, *I* can manage the whole lot of them! Impenetrability! That's what *I* say!"

"Would you tell me, please, what that means?"

"Now you talk like a reasonable child," said Humpty Dumpty, looking very much pleased. "I meant by 'impenetrability' that we've had enough of that subject, and it would be just as well if you'd mention what you mean to do next, as I suppose you don't mean to stop here all the rest of your life."

"That's a great deal to make one word mean," Alice said in a thoughtful tone.

"When I make a word do a lot of work like that," said Humpty Dumpty, "I always pay it extra."

Humpty Dumpty and Alice, *Looking-Glass*, Chap. 6, *Humpty Dumpty*

"I can explain all the poems that ever were invented – and a good many that haven't been invented just yet."

Humpty Dumpty to Alice, *Looking-Glass*,
Chap. 6, *Humpty Dumpty*

"You see, it's like a portmanteau – there are two meanings packed up into one word."

Humpty Dumpty to Alice, *Looking-Glass*,
Chap. 6, *Humpty Dumpty*

"If you tell me what language 'fiddle-de-dee' is, I'll tell you the French for it!" she exclaimed triumphantly.

But the Red Queen drew herself up rather stiffly, and said "Queens never make bargains."

Alice and the Red Queen, *Looking-Glass*,
Chap. 9, *Queen Alice*

"It's too late to correct it," said the Red Queen: "when you've once said a thing, that fixes it, and you must take the consequences."

The Red Queen to Alice, *Looking-Glass*,
Chap. 9, *Queen Alice*

"In winter, when the fields are white,
I sing this song for your delight –

only I don't sing it," he added, as an explanation.

"I see you don't" said Alice.

"If you can *see* whether I'm singing or not, you've sharper eyes than most," Humpty Dumpty remarked severely.

Humpty Dumpty and Alice, *Looking-Glass*,
Chap. 6, *Humpty Dumpty*

"I see nobody on the road," said Alice.

"I only wish *I* had such eyes," the King remarked in a fretful tone. "To be able to see Nobody! And at that distance too! Why, it's as much

as *I* can do to see real people, by this light!"
Alice and the White King, *Looking-Glass*,
Chap. 7, *The Lion and the Unicorn*

I told them once, I told them twice:
They would not listen to advice.
...
I said it very loud and clear:
I went and shouted in his ear.
But he was very stiff and proud:
He said, 'You needn't shout so loud!'
Humpty Dumpty to Alice, *Looking-Glass*,
Chap. 6, *Humpty Dumpty*

"It's as large as life,
and twice as natural!"

"If you do such a thing again, I'll have you
buttered! It went through and through my head
like an earthquake!"
The White King to Alice, *Looking-Glass*,
Chap. 7, *The Lion and the Unicorn*

"It's as large as life, and twice as natural!"
The Haigha to the Unicorn (describing Alice),
Looking-Glass,
Chap. 7, *The Lion and the Unicorn*

"It's my own invention."

At this moment her thoughts were interrupted by a loud shouting of "Ahoy! Ahoy! Check!" and a Knight, dressed in crimson armour, came galloping down upon her, brandishing a great club. Just as he reached her, the horse stopped suddenly: "You're my prisoner!" the Knight cried, as he tumbled off his horse.

> The Red Knight to Alice, *Looking-Glass*,
> Chap. 8, *"It's My Own Invention"*

"She's *my* prisoner, you know!" the Red Knight said at last.

"Yes, but then *I* came and rescued her!" the White Knight replied.

> The Red Knight and White Knight, *Looking-Glass*,
> Chap. 8, *"It's My Own Invention"*

"Yes, it's a very good beehive," the Knight said in a discontented tone, "one of the best kind. But not a single bee has come near it yet. And the other thing is a mousetrap. I suppose the mice keep the bees out – or the bees keep the mice out, I don't know which.

> The White Knight to Alice, *Looking-Glass*,
> Chap. 8, *"It's My Own Invention"*

"You see," he went on after a pause, "it's as well to be provided for *everything*. That's the reason the horse has all those anklets around his feet."

"But what are they for?" Alice asked in a tone of great curiosity.

"To guard against the bites of sharks," the Knight replied.

> The White Knight to Alice, *Looking-Glass,*
> Chap. 8, *"It's My Own Invention"*

"I hope you've got your hair well fastened on?" he continued, as they set off.

"Only in the usual way," Alice said, smiling.

"That's hardly enough," he said, anxiously. "You see, the wind is so *very* strong here. It's as strong as soup."

"Have you invented a plan for keeping the hair from being blown off?" Alice enquired.

"Not yet," said the Knight. "But I've got a plan for keeping it from *falling* off."

"I should like to hear it, very much."

"First you take an upright stick," said the Knight. "Then you make your hair creep up it, like a fruit tree. Now, the reason hair falls off is because it hangs *down* – things never fall *upwards*, you know. It's a plan of my own invention. You may try it if you like."

The White Knight and Alice, *Looking-Glass*, Chap. 8, *"It's My Own Invention"*

"I haven't tried it yet," the Knight said, gravely, "so I can't tell for certain – but I'm afraid it *would* be a little hard."

The White Knight to Alice, *Looking-Glass*, Chap. 8, *"It's My Own Invention"*

"How *can* you go on talking so quietly, head downwards?" Alice asked. ...

The Knight looked surprised at the question. "What does it matter where my body happens to be?" he said. "My mind goes on working all the same. In fact, the more head-downwards I am, the more I keep inventing new things."

Alice and the White Knight, *Looking-Glass*, Chap. 8, *"It's My Own Invention"*

"I don't believe that pudding ever *was* cooked! In fact, I don't believe that pudding ever *will* be cooked! And yet it was a very clever pudding to invent."

The White Knight to Alice, *Looking-Glass*,
Chap. 8, *"It's My Own Invention"*

**I'll tell you everything I can:
There's little to relate.**

*I'll tell you everything I can:
There's little to relate.*

The White Knight to Alice, *Looking-Glass*,
Chap. 8, *"It's My Own Invention"*

*He said 'I look for butterflies
That sleep among the wheat:
I make them into mutton pies,
And sell them in the street.'*

The White Knight to Alice, *Looking-Glass*,
Chap. 8, *"It's My Own Invention"*

*But I was thinking of a plan
To dye my whiskers green,
And always use so large a fan
That they could not be seen.*

The White Knight to Alice, *Looking-Glass*,
Chap. 8, *"It's My Own Invention"*

He said 'I go my ways,
And when I find a mountain rill,
I set it in a blaze.'
The White Knight to Alice, *Looking-Glass,*
Chap. 8, *"It's My Own Invention"*

But I was thinking of a way
To feed oneself on batter,
And so go on from day to day
Getting a little fatter.
The White Knight to Alice, *Looking-Glass,*
Chap. 8, *"It's My Own Invention"*

I shook him well from side to side,
Until his face was blue:
'Come, tell me how you live,' I cried,
'And what it is you do!'

He said 'I hunt for haddocks' eyes
Among the heather bright,
And work them into waistcoat buttons
In the silent night.'
The White Knight to Alice, *Looking-Glass,*
Chap. 8, *"It's My Own Invention"*

'I sometimes dig for buttered rolls,
Or set limed twigs for crabs:
I sometimes search the grassy knolls
For wheels of Hansom cabs.'
The White Knight to Alice, *Looking-Glass,*
Chap. 8, *"It's My Own Invention"*

And very gladly will I drink
Your Honour's noble health.
The White Knight to Alice, *Looking-Glass,*
Chap. 8, *"It's My Own Invention"*

**"I should *like*
to be a Queen, best."**

"Let's pretend we're kings and queens."
Alice, *Looking-Glass,*
Chap. 1, *Looking-Glass House*

Hush-a-by lady, in Alice's lap!
Till feast's ready, we've time for a nap.
When the feast's over, we'll go to the ball –
Red Queen, and White Queen, and Alice, and all!
The Red Queen, *Looking-Glass,*
Chap. 9, *Queen Alice*

Then fill up the glasses as quick as you can,
And sprinkle the table with buttons and bran:
Put cats in the coffee, and mice in the tea –
And welcome Queen Alice with thirty-times-three!

Then fill up the glasses with treacle and ink,
Or anything else that is pleasant to drink:
Mix sand with the cider, and wool with the wine –
And welcome Queen Alice with ninety-times-nine!
Voices at the feast,
Looking-Glass, Chap. 9,
Queen Alice

"It's a great huge game of chess that's being played – all over the world."
Alice, *Looking-Glass*, Chap. 2, *The Garden of Live Flowers*

"I wouldn't mind being a Pawn, if only I might join – though of course I should *like* to be a Queen, best."

Alice, *Looking-Glass*,
Chap. 2, *The Garden of Live Flowers*

"It'll never do for you to be lolling about on the grass like that! Queens have to be dignified, you know!"

Alice (scolding herself), *Looking-Glass*,
Chap. 9, *Queen Alice*

So she got up and walked about – rather stiffly just at first, as she was afraid that the crown might come off: but she comforted herself with the thought that there was nobody to see her, "and if I really am a Queen," she said as she sat down again, "I shall be able to manage it quite well in time."

Alice, *Looking-Glass*,
Chap. 9, *Queen Alice*

"Are you a child or a teetotum?"

"Are you a child or a teetotum?"
The Sheep to Alice, *Looking-Glass*,
Chap. 5, *Wool and Water*

I have not seen thy sunny face,
Nor heard thy silver laughter:

No thought of me shall find a place
In thy young life's hereafter
Looking-Glass,
Introduction

Without, the frost, the blinding snow,
The storm-wind's moody madness –
Within, the firelight's ruddy glow,
And childhood's nest of gladness.
Looking-Glass,
Introduction

"What do you suppose is the use of a child without any meaning? Even a joke should have some meaning – and a child's more important than a joke, I hope."
The Red Queen to Alice, *Looking-Glass,*
Chap. 9, *Queen Alice*

"Take a bone from a dog: what remains?"

Alice considered. "The bone wouldn't remain, of course, if I took it – and the dog wouldn't remain: it would come to bite me – and I'm sure *I* wouldn't remain!"

"Then you think nothing would remain?" said the Red Queen.

"I think that's the answer."

"Wrong, as usual," said the Red Queen: "the dog's temper would remain."

"But I don't see how – "

"Why, look here!" the Red Queen cried. "The dog would lose its temper, wouldn't it?"

"Perhaps it would," Alice replied cautiously.

"Then if the dog went away, its temper would remain!" the Queen exclaimed triumphantly.

> The Red Queen and Alice, *Looking-Glass*,
> Chap. 9, *Queen Alice*

"Do let's pretend that I'm a hungry hyaena, and you're a bone!"

> Alice, *Looking-Glass*,
> Chap. 1, *Looking-Glass House*

**"What dreadful nonsense
we *are* talking!"**

Alice sighed and gave it up. "It's exactly like a riddle with no answer!" she thought.

> Alice, *Looking-Glass*,
> Chap. 9, *Queen Alice*

"What tremendously easy riddles you ask!"

> Humpty Dumpty to Alice, *Looking-Glass*,
> Chap. 6, *Humpty Dumpty*

"Fan her head!" the Red Queen anxiously interrupted. "She'll be feverish after so much thinking."

> The Red Queen (about Alice), *Looking-Glass*,
> Chap. 9, *Queen Alice*

"Now, here, we mostly have days and nights two or three at a time, and sometimes in the winter we take as many as five nights together – for warmth, you know."

"Are five nights warmer than one night, then?" Alice ventured to ask.

"Five times as warm, of course."

"But they should be five times as *cold*, by the same rule –"

"Just so!" cried the Red Queen. "Five times as warm, *and* five times as cold – just as I'm five times as rich as you are, *and* five times as clever!"

The Red Queen and Alice, *Looking-Glass*,
Chap. 9, *Queen Alice*

"He said he would come in," the White Queen went on, "because he was looking for a hippopotamus. Now, as it happened, there wasn't such a thing in the house, that morning."

"Is there generally?" Alice asked in an astonished tone.

"Well, only on Thursdays," said the Queen.

The White Queen and Alice, *Looking-Glass*,
Chap. 9, *Queen Alice*

"Your Majesty must excuse her," the Red Queen said to Alice, taking one of the White Queen's hands in her own, and gently stroking it: "she means well, but she can't help saying foolish things as a general rule."

The Red Queen to Alice, *Looking-Glass*,
Chap. 9, *Queen Alice*

She couldn't help thinking to herself "What dreadful nonsense we *are* talking!"

Alice, *Looking-Glass*,
Chap. 9, *Queen Alice*

The white kitten had had nothing to do with it.

One thing was certain, that the *white* kitten had had nothing to do with it – it was the black kitten's fault entirely.

Looking-Glass,
Chap. 1, *Looking-Glass House*

It is a very inconvenient habit of kittens (Alice had once made the remark) that, whatever you say to them, they *always* purr. "If they would only purr for 'yes' and mew for 'no,' or any rule of that sort," she had said, "so that one could keep up a conversation! But how *can* you talk with a person if they *always* say the same thing?"

Alice, *Looking-Glass*,
Chap. 9, *Queen Alice*

Life, what is it but a dream?

"He's dreaming now," said Tweedledee: "and what do you think he's dreaming about?" Alice said "Nobody can guess that."

"Why, about *you!*" Tweedledee exclaimed, clapping his hands triumphantly. "And if he left off dreaming about you, where do you suppose you'd be?"

"Where I am now, of course," said Alice.

"Not you!" Tweedledee retorted contemptuously. "You'd be nowhere. Why, you're only a sort of thing in his dream!"

"If that there King was to awake," added Tweedledum, "you'd go out – bang! – just like a candle!"

Tweedledee and Tweedledum to Alice, *Looking-Glass*,
Chap. 4, *Tweedledum and Tweedledee*

"Oh, *what* a lovely one! Only I couldn't quite reach it" And it certainly *did* seem a little provoking ("almost as if it happened on purpose," she thought) that, though she managed to pick plenty of beautiful rushes as the boat glided by, there was always a more lovely one that she couldn't reach.

"The prettiest are always further!"

Alice, *Looking-Glass*,
Chap. 5, *Wool and Water*

"So I wasn't dreaming, after all," she said to herself, "unless – unless we're all part of the same dream. Only I do hope it's *my* dream, and not the Red King's! I don't like belonging to another person's dream."

Alice, *Looking-Glass*,
Chap. 8, *"It's My Own Invention"*

Long has paled that sunny sky:
Echoes fade and memories die:
Autumn frosts have slain July.

Still she haunts me, phantomwise.
Alice moving under skies
Never seen by waking eyes

Ever drifting down the stream –
Lingering in the golden gleam –
Life, what is it but a dream?

Looking-Glass,
Chap. 9, *Queen Alice*

Index

Lewis Carroll

Lewis Carroll was born Charles Lutwidge Dodgson in 1832 near the village of Daresbury, England, the son of an Anglican minister and the oldest boy in a family of four boys and seven girls. He attended Rugby (infamous as the school of Thomas Hughes, author of *Tom Brown's School Days*, and later of George MacDonald Fraser's fictional adventurer-cad, Harry Flashman), then went on to study and later lecture in mathematics at Oxford University.

He was ordained as an Anglican deacon, and so became the Rev. Dodgson, but never fully became a priest. (For several reasons. Among them, he loved the theatre, which the church still frowned on, and he had both a partial hearing loss and a speech impediment, which made preaching difficult.) He never married (Alexander Woollcott aptly describes him as a "gentle, shrinking celibate") and he spent most of his adult life in bachelor rooms as a don at the college of Christ Church.

He was fussy, prim, eccentric and brilliant, a talented amateur photographer and a prolific writer — hundreds of poems, letters and essays on topics as varied as Euclidian geometry, animal research and the art of writing letters. (Always stamp and address the envelope first, he advises. By his own meticulous log, kept over the course of 37 years, by the time of his death in 1898, he'd written 98,721 letters.)

But it's for the Alice books we most remember him. Typically, each began as a story told to entertain a young girl. Painfully shy and awkward around adults, with children Dodgson became relaxed and himself childlike, and even lost his stammer.

Although his preference for children, especially young girls, may have been a bit odd, it also appears to have been entirely innocent. When photographing children, he made sure the child's mother or another chaperone was present, none of his child friends ever suggested anything improper had ever happened in any of their time spent together, he remained on good terms with many of his child friends even after they grew up, and they spoke of him fondly. There's no evidence to suggest it was anything more insidious (if somewhat sad) than a desire to recapture, even if only momentarily, his own childhood innocence. (There's also no evidence, as some have at times suggested, that his fantastic imagination owed anything to the use of opium or any other drugs or artificial stimulants.)

For the sake of propriety and because he was a very private man, even long before the Alice books, Dodgson had already begun using the pen name Lewis Carroll for his fanciful literary works (as opposed to his serious mathematical ones). He chose it with typical ingenuity by reversing his first two names and tinkering with them in French and Latin, and maybe a little German. (By the same means, he'd also considered using Louis Carroll or Edgar Cuthwellis.)

Bits of the author appear all through the Alice books. His birthplace of Daresbury is in the county of Cheshire, hence the Cheshire Cat. Like the White Rabbit, he was meticulous in the way he dressed, right down to the white gloves. Like the White Knight, he was always inventing things, not all of them practical or useful. Like the Mad Hatter, he loved puzzles and riddles. And he shared with Humpty Dumpty a fascination for, and a complete mastery of, words and language. He's even there by surname in *Wonderland* as the Dodo in Chapter 3, who presents Alice with the "elegant thimble" after the Caucus-Race. (By his own stammering pronunciation, Do-Do-Dodgson becomes Dodo.)

Carroll wrote other fictional works, including the epic nonsense poem *The Hunting of the Snark* (for which, with typical ingenuity, he was the first to suggest the use of book dustjackets) and the children's books *Sylvie and Bruno* and *Sylvie and Bruno Concluded.*

Of course, none of them has ever reached the popularity, or the enduring appeal, of the two Alice books. And of course, any way you look at it, the Alice books alone should be more than enough of a legacy.

About the Editor

David W. Barber is a journalist and musician and the author of nine books of musical history and humor, including *Bach, Beethoven and the Boys*, *When the Fat Lady Sings*, and *Tutus, Tights and Tiptoes*. Formerly entertainment editor of the Kingston, Ont., *Whig-Standard* and editor of *Broadcast Week* magazine at the Toronto *Globe and Mail*, he's now a freelance journalist and musician in Toronto. As a composer, his works include two symphonies, a jazz mass based on the music of Dave Brubeck, a *Requiem*, several short choral and chamber works and various vocal-jazz songs and arrangements. He sings with the Toronto Chamber Choir and with his vocal-jazz group, Barber & the Sevilles, which has released a CD, called *Cybersex*.

First published in Canada by
Quotable Books
an imprint of
Sound And Vision
359 Riverdale Avenue
Toronto, Canada M4J 1A4

http://www.soundandvision.com
E-mail: musicbooks@soundandvision.com
First edition, August 2001
1 3 5 7 9 11 13 15 - printings - 14 12 10 8 6 4 2

National Library of Canada
Cataloguing in Publication Data
Carroll, Lewis, 1832-1898
Quotable Alice
(*Quotable Books*)
ISBN 0-920151-52-3
1. Carroll, Lewis, 1832-1898—Quotations.
2. Alice (Fictitious character : Carroll)—Quotations.
3. Quotations, English. I. Barber, David W.
(David William), 1958- II. Title. III. Series.

PR4612.A2 2001   823'.   C2001-902003-1

Cover illustration by Kevin Reeves
Jacket design by Jim Stubbington
Typeset in Century Schoolbook

Printed and bound in Canada

By David W. Barber, cartoons by Dave Donald

A Musician's Dictionary
preface by Yehudi Menuhin
isbn 0-920151-21-3

Bach, Beethoven and the Boys
Music History as it Ought to Be Taught
preface by Anthony Burgess
isbn 0-920151-10-8

When the Fat Lady Sings
Opera History as it Ought to Be Taught
preface by Maureen Forrester
foreword by Anna Russell
isbn 0-920151-34-5

If it Ain't Baroque
More Music History as it Ought to Be Taught
isbn 0-920151-15-9

Getting a Handel on Messiah
preface by Trevor Pinnock
isbn 0-920151-17-5

Tenors, Tantrums and Trills
An Opera Dictionary from Aida to Zzzz
isbn 0-920151-19-1

Tutus, Tights and Tiptoes
Ballet History as it Ought to Be Taught
preface by Karen Kain
isbn 0-920151-30-2

By David W. Barber (editor)

Better Than It Sounds
A Dictionary of Humorous Musical Quotations
isbn 0-920151-22-1

A *Quotable Book*
Quotable Sherlock
illustrations by Sidney Paget
isbn 0-920151-52-1

Other books from Sound And Vision and
Quotable Books

Love Lives of the Great Composers
From Gesualdo to Wagner
by Basil Howitt
isbn 0-920151-18-3

How to Stay Awake
During Anybody's Second Movement
by David E. Walden
cartoons by Mike Duncan
preface by Charlie Farquharson
isbn 0-920151-20-5

A Working Musician's Joke Book
by Daniel G. Theaker
cartoons by Mike Freen
preface by David W. Barber
isbn 0-920151-23-X

The Composers
A Hystery of Music
by Kevin Reeves
preface by Daniel Taylor
isbn 0-920151-29-9

How To Listen To Modern Music
Without Earplugs
by David E. Walden
cartoons by Mike Duncan
foreword by Bramwell Tovey
isbn 0-920151-31-0

The Thing I've Played With the Most
Professor Anthon E. Darling Discusses
His Favourite Instrument
by David E. Walden
cartoons by Mike Duncan
foreword by Mabel May Squinnge, B.O.
isbn 0-920151-35-3

116

Opera Antics & Anecdotes
by Stephen Tanner
illustrations by Umberto Tàccola
foreword by David W. Barber
isbn 0-920151-31-0

I Wanna Be Sedated
Pop Music in the Seventies
by Phil Dellio & Scott Woods
caricatures by Dave Prothero
preface by Chuck Eddy
isbn 0-920151-16-7

a *Quotable Book*
Quotable Pop
Five Decades of Blah Blah Blah
by Phil Dellio & Scott Woods
caricatures by Mike Rooth
isbn 0-920151-50-7

a *Quotable Book*
Quotable Opera
by Steve Tanner
illustrations by Umberto Tàccola
isbn 0-920151-54-X

A Note from the Publisher

Sound And Vision is pleased to announce the creation of a new imprint called *Quotable Books.* The first three in the series are illustrated on the back cover. Other titles planned include *Quotable Shakespeare, Twain, Poe, Wilde, Blake, Dickens.* The series will cover the arts, *Quotable Opera, Jazz,* and *Heavy Metal* plus literature and other subject areas, including politicians and statesmen such as Winston Churchill, Oliver Cromwell and Abraham Lincoln.

Our books may be purchased for educational or promotional use or for special sales. If you have any comments on this book or any other book we publish or if you would like a catalogue, please write to us at:

Sound And Vision,
359 Riverdale Avenue,
Toronto, Canada M4J 1A4.

Visit our web site at: www.soundandvision.com. We would really like to hear from you.

We are always looking for suitable original books to publish. If you have an idea or manuscript, please contact us.

Thank you for purchasing or borrowing this book.

Geoffrey Savage
Publisher